The Four Seasons

It's Summer

Alana Olsen

illustrated by
Aurora Aguilera

PowerKiDS
press.

New York

Published in 2017 by The Rosen Publishing Group, Inc.
29 East 21st Street, New York, NY 10010

First Edition

Managing Editor: Nathalie Beullens-Maoui
Editor: Sarah Machajewski
Book Design: Michael Flynn
Illustrator: Aurora Aguilera

Cataloging-in-Publication Data

Names: Olsen, Alana.
Title: It's summer / Alana Olsen.
Description: New York : Powerkids Press, 2016. | Series: The four seasons | Includes index.
Identifiers: ISBN 9781508151876 (pbk.) | ISBN 9781508151890 (library bound) | ISBN 9781508151883 (6 pack)
Subjects: LCSH: Summer–Juvenile literature.
Classification: LCC QB637.6 O47 2016 | DDC 508.2–dc23

Manufactured in the United States of America

CPSIA Compliance Information: Batch #BS16PK: For Further Information contact Rosen Publishing, New York, New York at 1-800-237-9932

Contents

Today, I'm going to wear my bathing suit. It's finally summer!

It's very hot outside.

Dad says we can go to the beach.

I pack my towel for swimming.

I pack my flip-flops for walking
on hot sand.

It's very sunny.

Mom reminds me to wear sunglasses.

There are many people at
the beach. Some people swim.
Other people play volleyball.

13

I put sunscreen on.

It keeps my skin safe under
the summer sun.

15

My sister and I build
a sand castle.

16

It's almost as tall as I am!

18

My friend Ravi is swimming.
My mom says I can swim, too.

I run into the water to join Ravi.

We jump into the waves.

We go home when
the sun sets.

The beach is my favorite place
in summer!

Words to Know

flip-flops

sand castle

sunscreen

Index

24